This book is dedicated
to my family.

LONDON BOROUGH OF WANDSWORTH	
9030 00002 4052 0	
Askews & Holts	14-Jun-2012
JF	£6.99
	WWX0009395/0032

a templar book

First published in the UK in hardback in 2010 by Templar Publishing,
this softback edition published in 2012 by Templar Publishing,
an imprint of The Templar Company Limited,
The Granary, North Street, Dorking, Surrey,
RH4 1DN, UK
www.templarco.co.uk

First softback edition

ISBN 978-1-84877-132-1

Printed in China

foxly's FEAST

OWEN DAVEY

RECIPES

templar publishing

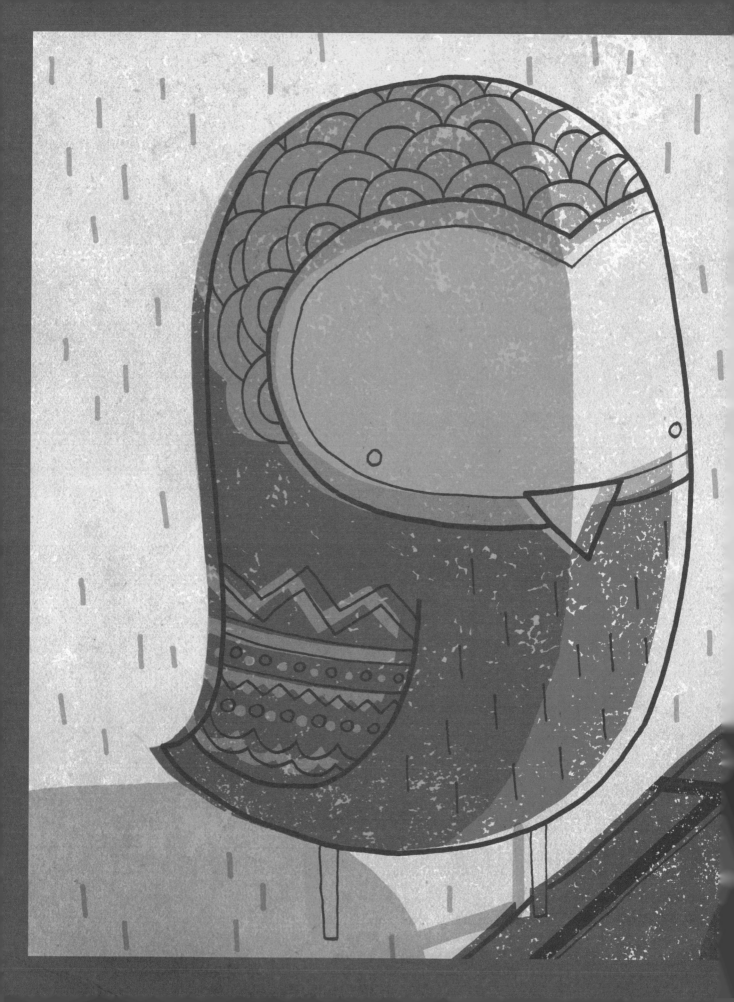